The Littlest Pumpkin

Written by
Brandi Dougherty

Illustrated by
Denise Hughes

Cartwheel Books
An Imprint of Scholastic Inc.
New York

For my friends and longtime critique partners,
Susan B. Katz and Evan Sagerman — B.D.

For Sam and Will — D.H.

Petey was a pumpkin.
He lived with his family in the Spooky Woods pumpkin patch.
There were many pumpkins in Petey's patch,

but Petey was the littlest one.

It was almost Halloween, and Petey's seeds swirled with excitement.

This year, he was finally big enough to participate in the pumpkin decorating contest at the Halloween bash.

HALLOWEEN BASH
PUMPKIN DECORATING
CONTEST

Petey just knew he would be chosen for the contest.
After all, his great-grandma Squash once won
the "Spookiest" award three years in a row!

Petey's mom helped him polish up his skin until it was bright orange and super shiny.
Petey's sister, Portia, made his stem look just right.
"You're so cute!" she gushed.

PUMPKIN POLISH

Petey frowned.
He didn't want to look cute.
He wanted to look big and spooky!

Soon, families from all over the Spooky Woods came to the pumpkin patch.
Some found their special pumpkin right away.
Others took their time, examining lots of different pumpkins.
Portia was one of the right-away pumpkins.
"See you at the party!" she called.

Petey put on his best "pick me" smile when two monsters wandered over.

"What about this one?" one monster said, pointing to Petey.

Petey held his breath.

The other monster shook his head. "Too little."

Later that day, Petey practiced some spooky *boos* with his dad.

"A little louder," his dad coached.

"Boo!" Petey shouted.

"Bless you," a vampire responded, thinking Petey had sneezed.

Before he could try *boo* again, the vampire picked up his dad! "This one's perfectly spooky."

"See you soon, Son!" his dad said with a chuckle.

The next morning, Petey heard an ogre looking for a bumpy pumpkin.

Petey quickly rolled through some leaves hoping to appear bigger and bumpier, but instead, he got lost in the pile!

Next, Petey used a wheelbarrow to hop onto a fence post. *Up here, I'll be noticed for sure,* he thought.

"Look at that pumpkin, Gran!" a werepup barked.
"That's too little, Wendel," his gran replied, steering him
in the other direction.

The crowds came and went, but Petey stayed.

"There's always next year," Petey's mom reassured him.
Just then, a ghost picked her up.
"Look at this big one," the ghost said to her family
as they drifted away.
"See you tonight, Love!" Petey's mom shouted down to him.
"And don't worry!"

Petey slowly rolled through the pumpkin patch.
A tear splashed in the dirt in front of him.
Everyone wanted a different type of pumpkin.
Nobody wanted the littlest one.

Just then, Petey heard two girls talking.
He stopped and watched a witch and a mummy stroll his way.
They were little — just like Petey!

"Mae, look at that pumpkin!" the witch said to her friend.
"This one, Wilma?" the mummy asked, gently picking up Petey.
He didn't try to make himself look spooky or bumpy or big.
He just smiled.

"He's perfect!" Wilma and Mae said together.

The girls took Petey home and decorated his skin with special glowing paint. He loved the spooky design.

"We're ready for the pumpkin contest!" they cheered.

Petey, Wilma, and Mae were the first ones at the party. Petey beamed as his family arrived one by one. There was just one problem.

"Why aren't you decorated, Portia?" Petey asked his sister.
"I'm too scared to be in the pumpkin contest," she told Petey.
"What if no one likes me?"
Petey looked at Wilma and Mae and smiled. He had an idea.

With Wilma and Mae's help, Petey got to work decorating Portia with glowing paint just like his.

When they made it back to their table, the contest had begun. Petey balanced on Portia's head to complete their design.

The judges loved the double-painted pumpkins —
one big and one little.
They gave the new friends a ribbon for "Best Team Effort."

Petey had a blast at the Halloween bash.
He got to watch Wilma in a high-flying broom routine and
Mae in a fun mummy dance. And they ate enough treats to
last them all the way until next year.

It was fun to feel a little spooky sometimes,
but Petey was happiest being himself.
And that little idea was the biggest joy of all!